# Words On Wings

By Barbara Williamson

To order additional copies of this book, contact:
Xlibris
844-714-8691
www.Xlibris.com
Orders@Xlibris.com

ISBN:   Softcover            978-1-4363-3531-7
        Hardcover            978-1-6641-8371-1
        EBook                978-1-4771-8124-9

Library of Congress Control Number: 2008903320

Print information available on the last page

Rev. date: 07/06/2021

This story is dedicated to my precious Mother-in-law, Sylvia, who inspired me to write about acts of kindness. Her smile warms my heart, and her loving words always comfort me.

Prayers are powerful. Friends are gifts sent to encourage and give support until our prayers are answered. Thank you to my family and friends that made this story a token of my appreciation for Mom.

Do you believe in Angels? Perhaps, after you read this story about an Angel whom I know, you will believe in Angels, too.

The Angel's name is Sylvia Genevieve. She lives in a little brown house on the shore of Little Sand Lake. To most people that know her, Miss Sylvia is the sweet, elderly woman who is always smiling. Visitors are always welcome in her home. There is always coffee brewing, nice cold milk to drink, and something sweet to share.

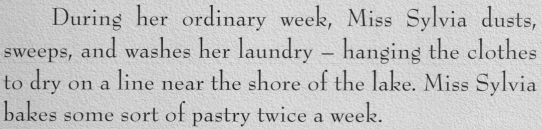

During her ordinary week, Miss Sylvia dusts, sweeps, and washes her laundry – hanging the clothes to dry on a line near the shore of the lake. Miss Sylvia bakes some sort of pastry twice a week.

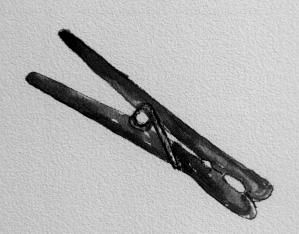

The favorite part of Miss Sylvia's day, however, is walking to her mailbox to check for postcards. Miss Sylvia has been collecting postcards for over thirty years. She has received postcards from all over the world. She has joyfully said, "I have ventured out all over the world, while sitting right here in my cozy rocker. I have been blessed by many well-wishers sending nice thoughts, while visiting beautiful places. I am so grateful."

Miss Sylvia walks to her mailbox six days a week, every week, unless there is a holiday. She counted her steps one morning and found that it takes 3,130 steps to walk from her house, to find her treasures, and to return home. Let me explain, Miss Sylvia refers to her postcards as her treasures — she has received and saved over 4,000 throughout the years.

As Miss Sylvia walks to the mailbox, she prays. She prays for her family, friends, and the friends she would meet someday. Miss Sylvia also prays for a way to share the love that she has been so blessed to receive from all the postcard senders.

Miss Sylvia stores her postcards in shoeboxes. She keeps the boxes stacked one on top of another. All the boxes are stored in her basement. On many days, she sits by her window looking out on the grassy side of her yard, revisiting her treasures that she has looked at so many times before.

One warm, summer day, Miss Sylvia opened all the windows in her house to cool her house down, and to allow the sounds of the birds to be heard throughout the house. As the day wore on, a breeze picked up and it looked like it was going to rain. She closed the windows upstairs, but forgot about the basement windows.

When Miss Sylvia finished her chores for the day, she poured herself a cup of coffee and sat in her favorite chair – the one near the window overlooking the lake. It had been a rather busy day already, but she decided to write a letter to her sister, Lil, before making dinner. She finished the letter, placed a stamp in the corner of the envelope, and set it on the table next to the door. She heated some Swedish sausage and boiled some potatoes for dinner. After dinner she looked through some of her family photographs, before heading off to bed – she was still thinking about her sister.

That night while Miss Sylvia slept, the wind blew through the basement windows.  As it blew, it carried some of her postcards right out one of the windows. Then, it did rain and the postcards that had blown out the window were, now, completely wet.

The following afternoon, when the sun was shinning, the strangest thing happened – the most beautiful flowers began to bloom where the wet postcards lodged in the grass.  Now, these were no ordinary flowers; these flowers had blossoms in the shape of hearts!

The next day, when Miss Sylvia went out to mow the lawn, she came around the south side of her house and saw the beautiful flowers. When she bent down to get a closer look at the unexpected and magical flowers, she realized that they were coming from the postcards.

While on her knees, Miss Sylvia began to pray. She prayed, "My precious Lord, thank you for these beautiful flowers from the wonderful postcards. Please send a way for me to share these lovely thoughts with people who are sad or lonely or not feeling well. I want to share my treasures. I trust in you, Lord, for an idea! Amen."

The next morning on her walk to the mailbox, Miss Sylvia saw a scruffy looking crow, bobbing from tree to tree. She said, "Good morning, Mr. Crow. Are you the answer to my prayer? I hope you know it might be a big job!" The crow followed Miss Sylvia, watching her as he continued to bob along.

As Miss Sylvia arrived at her mailbox, the crow flew over to her and sat right on the top of it. As she opened her mailbox, he just watched her. She gave him a little news flyer that was with her other mail. Then, he flew away.

Miss Sylvia turned and started to walk back towards her house, with three new postcards in her hand. As she came around the corner of her garage, she saw the crow sitting on her porch with the flyer right beside him.

"My, my, Mr. Crow, maybe you are the answer to my prayer," said Miss Sylvia. "Okay, from now on your name is Bob, since you like to "bob" from tree to tree. Now, just wait here Bob, I'll be right back," she said. She returned with some nice raisin cookies and gave Bob one, while she ate the other one. Then, she read her postcards to Bob.

One of the cards was a picture of a beautiful lake with a caption that read, "Wish you were here." On the back of the card was written, "May God send you a beautiful day. Please know that He loves you." Just then, Miss Sylvia thought of her friend, Margaret, who used to live at the lake. Margaret now lives in a small apartment in the big city, miles away.

Miss Sylvia looked at Bob and said, "If I tell you exactly where my friend lives in the city, do you think that you could deliver something to her?" Bob nodded his head and winked an eye to let Miss Sylvia know that he could do the job. "How wonderful!" said Miss Sylvia. Then she said, "Okay, Bob, you meet me here tomorrow morning. I will feed you breakfast and, then, send you on your way."

That night Miss Sylvia pondered ideas for sending a special greeting to Margaret, and other people needing some uplifting thoughts and words. Then it came to her, why not resend the gifts of kindness in her postcard collection? She had happily received them the first time, so even better to give them again, she thought. She figured she could coordinate the thoughts and words for each person, and Bob could fly the cards to the recipients. She would decorate each card with a heart, over the place where her name and address appeared, and would simply sign the card, "Words On Wings." If this works out, she thought, she and Bob could spread plenty of joy to plenty of people. Miss Sylvia prayed before she went to bed, thanking God for sending her a little "angel" in a scruffy crow suit.

The next morning Miss Sylvia woke up early and went to check if Bob was on her porch. There he was, sleeping on her wooden bench. She did not wake him, but went back in the house to cook a nice breakfast for him. She served Bob oatmeal brulee with wheat berries, and yummy cranberry cookies.

When Miss Sylvia went back out to the porch, Bob was wide-awake. She carried a tray with his breakfast, and a cup of coffee and a cookie for herself. Miss Sylvia set the tray down. Bob bobbed right over and began to eat. "STOP! I'll say a prayer before you begin to eat,"she said.

Bob waited patiently while Miss Sylvia prayed. When she had finished, Bob began to enjoy his cereal, and she explained to him how to fly to her friend Margret's house. "Now, Bob, you cannot just put the postcard in her mailbox. You need to set it right in front of her door," she explained. Although Bob was busy eating, he heard every word.

When Bob finished his meal, Miss Sylvia handed him the postcard signed "Words On Wings." She patted Bob's head and prayed, "God speed my dear Bob." Then Bob, the crow, flew away.

My Angel, Miss Sylvia, smiled all day long, thinking of her friend, Margaret, and the surprise she was about to receive. Miss Sylvia sang as she did her chores. She sang all the way to her mailbox, and found new postcards waiting for her there! Miss Sylvia read them on her walk back to her house. Her heart was jumping with joy as she thought about the next "Words On Wings" recipient. That afternoon, my Angel canned some fruit, made some goulash, and made a batch of raisin cookies — the kind Bob likes best.

As Miss Sylvia went about her day, she continued to think about her idea for sharing warm loving greetings with dear people. She thought about the sermon on Sunday at church, about loving others more then yourself. While thinking about this, she began to pray. "Thank you, Lord, you have blessed me with the idea of the gift of giving back," she whispered.

Each Sunday at church, Miss Sylvia writes down all the prayer requests and all the praise reports spoken during the service. She decided to use the names mentioned for her "Words On Wings" postcard project. From last Sunday there were:

♥ Nancy G. – prayers for my children's futures. And for me, may the Lord open my eyes and heart to serve Him;

♥ Sue F. – for friends to fellowship with;

♥ Elinor W. – prayers for Teresa;

♥ Marie M. – thanksgiving prayers for a wonderful marriage and family;

♥ Linda R. – for Clancey the Clown;

♥ Sue W. and Shelly – prayers for children;

♥ Alice G. – peace for Sarina; and

♥ Hank W. – patience and compassion for the entire world.

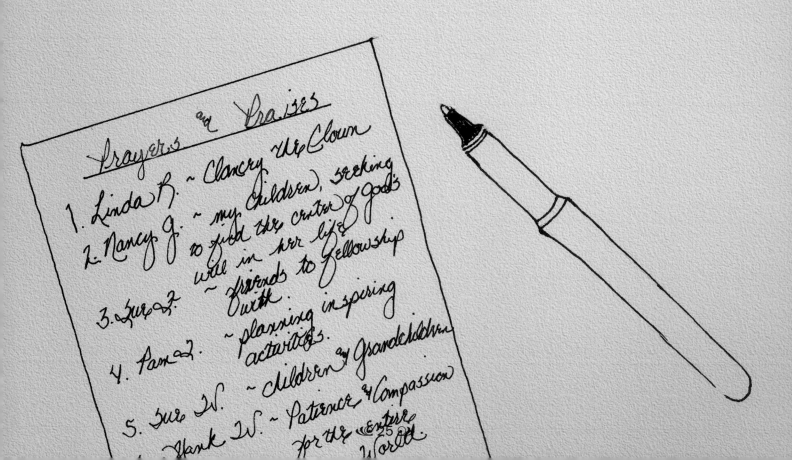

The following day she woke up early, put on a pot of coffee, and then went to check on Bob. There he was, waiting on the step. She said, "Good morning, Bob! Wait right here. I have some nice cookies for you." When Miss Sylvia went back in the house, the telephone started to ring. She picked up the receiver and said, "Hello, hello." It was her friend, Margaret, who wanted to tell her about a prayer that was wonderfully answered. Margaret said she had been praying, sharing with God how much she missed her old house at the lake. Then, instead of feeling sorry for herself, she thought it would be a good idea to go for a walk, and to be thankful for where she was. When she opened the door to go out, there, on the little rug by her front door, was a beautiful postcard with a picture of a lake. On the back of the card was written, "May God send you a beautiful day," she said.

"WOW!" said Miss Sylvia.

"Yes, WOW!" said Margaret. Because it was signed "Words On Wings," she said.

They talked a while longer on the telephone, then said goodbye. Miss Sylvia went outside and hugged Bob. "Wow, praise the Lord, we did it!" said Miss Sylvia. She returned to her kitchen and prepared a feast for Bob. This time Bob waited for Miss Sylvia to pray before he ate.

While Bob ate his breakfast, Miss Sylvia prepared the next postcard for him to deliver. As she painted a heart over her name and address, she smiled because she realized what Margaret meant when she said, "Yes, WOW!" The initials for "Words On Wings" are W-O-W.

The next Sunday at church, Miss Sylvia again listened to the prayer requests and praise reports. She made her list and thanked God again for this gift. This is what she wrote:

- ♥ Martie W. – children's Salvation;
- ♥ Gin K. – prayers for her sister, Earleen;
- ♥ Pam T. – organizing inspiring activities;
- ♥ Pat K. – a garden full of flowers to give away;
- ♥ Cheryl. B. – thanking God for her life and may she live her life for God;
- ♥ Peg K. – love and prayers for her sister Shril; and
- ♥ Bonnie K. – that my beloved and departed children, Jennifer and Jason, are being watched over in Heaven.

As Miss Sylvia listened to the prayers and praises, she knew that all the words spoken were from loving hearts. She also knew that the only One to answer these prayers is God. She felt like God put on her heart a sweet way to bring a little joy to people's lives.

The following Monday, Miss Sylvia received four lovely postcards in the mail. One read, "You are forever in my prayers." Another, "I think of you often, and wish you well." The next, "Please know you are being prayed for daily," and the last, "Love and good wishes to you." She smiled looking upward.

"Dear Lord, I know exactly where to put these new "WOW" cards. I will review my prayer list and send them out with Bob as soon as I can. Thank you, Lord," she smiled.

At the beginning of this story, I told you that I know an Angel. The dictionary description of an Angel is "a guardian spirit, a guiding influence, or a kind and loveable person."

Now that you know my story of an Angel, perhaps you would like to rethink about some of the people in your life. A mother or father, a grandmother or grandfather, a sister or brother, or a friend may be an Angel. I believe Angels surround us and may have many forms. Sometimes they are teachers, doctors, soldiers, firefighters, police officers, pastors, coaches, editors, or neighbors – people making loving differences in other people's lives. Their wings and halos are masked by open hands, inviting eyes, kind words of encouragement, caring conversation, and giving hearts.

I believe Angels are precious souls who think of others before they think of themselves. They give more then they receive. Angels do nice things for others without ever wanting or expecting to be thanked. I truly believe if the world were filled with more Miss Sylvia's, that it would be a sweeter place to live.

My prayer request: May our Lord keep putting Angels here on earth.

Love and Blessings!

Printed in the United States
by Baker & Taylor Publisher Services